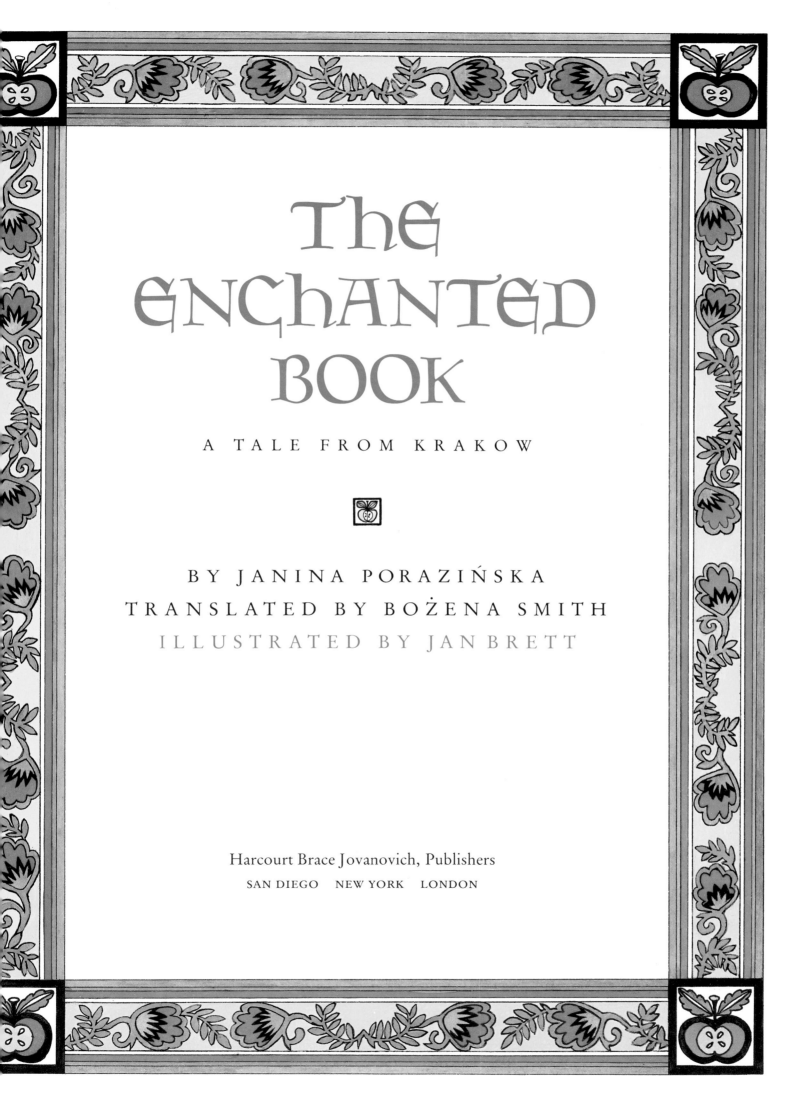

THE
ENCHANTED
BOOK

A TALE FROM KRAKOW

BY JANINA PORAZIŃSKA
TRANSLATED BY BOŻENA SMITH
ILLUSTRATED BY JAN BRETT

Harcourt Brace Jovanovich, Publishers

SAN DIEGO   NEW YORK   LONDON

Requests for permission to make copies of
any part of the work should be mailed to:
Permissions, Harcourt Brace Jovanovich, Publishers,
Orlando, Florida 32887.

Library of Congress Cataloging-in-Publication Data

Porazińska, Janina.
The enchanted book.

Translated from Polish.
Summary: A retelling of the traditional Polish tale
in which the youngest miller's daughter succeeds
in outwitting an evil sorcerer.
[1. Fairy tales. 2. Folklore—Poland]
I. Smith, Bożena. II. Brett, Jan, 1949–   ill. III. Title.
PZ8.1.P86En 1987   398.2′1′09438 [E]   86-22918
ISBN 0-15-225950-3

Printed in the United States of America
First edition
A B C D E

The paintings in this book were done in watercolor on Strathmore paper.

Illustration backgrounds were airbrushed by Joseph Hearne.

The text type was set in Stempel Garamond by Thompson Type, San Diego, California.

The display type was set in Goudy Mediaeval by Thompson Type, San Diego, California.

Color separations were made by Bright Arts (H.K.) Ltd., Hong Kong.

Printed by Rae Publishing, Cedar Grove, New Jersey

Bound by A. Horowitz & Sons, Bookbinders, Fairfield, New Jersey

Designed by Michael Farmer

Production supervision by Warren Wallerstein and Eileen McGlone

For my daughter, Maia.
          —B.S.

For Lia.
          —J. B.

A milldam, then a pond,
At pond's edge a mill.
The water flows along,
Mill wheels never still.
Mill wheel big, mill wheel small,
The miller's daughters—beauties all.

Like rosebuds were the miller's daughters, each one more beautiful than the others.

And there were three of them.

The eldest one had hair black as a raven's wing and a face as fair as if it had never seen sunlight. To stay pale she kept out of the sun.

They laughed at her in the village, and a song was written about her:

"Shady groves she seeks,
Woods of moss and fern.
She hides from the sun,
Afraid that she might burn."

The middle sister had hair red as the leaf of the beech tree and eyes green as waters running deep.

And the third sister was golden-haired, with eyes blue as flax blossoms. With her rosy glow, she seemed to have just descended from the clouds in fair weather, bringing the azure blue of the sky and the sunlit blush of dawn.

Each one had a different beauty, and each one wanted different things in life.

The eldest one wanted only to look beautiful. She constantly gazed at her reflection in a looking glass, in the water of the pond, and in the enthralled eyes of her admirers. She constantly asked herself and others, "Do I look pretty with this wreath of flowers in my hair? Or maybe this scarf would be lovelier? Should I pin my braids on top of my head, or let them hang to my waist? What looks more becoming around my neck, a string of amber or a strand of beads?"

The middle one wanted only to play, only to dance. Neither work was on her mind, nor her mother's good advice. She went from wedding feast to wedding feast, from celebration to celebration, from party to party.

The shepherd boy, the village wit, wrote a song about her:

"My head aches, my legs ache,
I can't do any work,
No work.
But singing and dancing,
I'll come help,
I'll help!"

And the youngest sister was interested in every kind of work.

"How do you get the thread you spin to come out so fine, so even? Teach me all about it! Mother, wake me up at sunrise at bread-making time, so I can learn to knead the dough. Father, let me ride to town alone to buy new screens for the mill. You have no sons, so a daughter must learn to drive the horses."

That's what the miller's three daughters were like.

Late autumn had come, foreshadowing winter. Heavy clouds gathered in the sky, wind whistled in bare branches, and the earth, stripped of her greenery, drenched by rain, seemed inhospitable to every living thing.

An old beggar woman knocked at the mill. Thin and frail she was, hungry, and cold through and through.

The miller's family took pity on her. They gave her a seat by the stove, and they gave her hot soup to eat.

The grandmother ate awhile and then said, "And now, good people, sit yourselves down, and listen while I read how it was centuries ago, ages ago."

The old woman dug around in her pack and pulled out a book fastened shut with a strap.

Everyone was extremely surprised that a beggar woman could read like a scholar. As long as the mill had been standing, no one so learned had yet been there!

Immediately the youngest daughter got up, fetched a clean cloth from the linen chest, and spread it out on the grandmother's lap.

And the old woman put some tobacco in her mouth, opened the book, and began to read.

She read about the twins, two sons of a forester's wife, who were stolen

out of their mother's crib. A she-wolf raised one, a she-bear raised the other. The brothers grew up, one with wolf cubs in the deep woods, the other with bear cubs in a forest den. The first one was suckled by the she-wolf on wolf's milk, the second by the she-bear on bear's milk. And they grew into immense giants, the likes of which hadn't been seen or heard of before.

One of them walked through the woods saying, "It looks like the grass didn't grow well this summer, for it barely comes up to my knees."

He was referring to pines, lindens, and birches.

If a house stood in his way, he'd merely lift his leg and step over it.

When one of the brothers wished a close look at a cow, he'd set it on the palm of his hand and lift it to his eyes like a kitten.

That's what the two giants were like.

One was named Oak-uprooter, the other Cliff-smasher, and they walked this earth setting things aright.

Oak-uprooter pulled up oaks and pines from the Tucholski Forest, carried them on his back like a bundle of kindling, and planted them in the Niepolomicka Wilderness, for every king who sat on the throne in Wawel Castle wanted thick oak woods and rustling pine forests near the royal city of Krakow. In these woods the kings bred game—bison, buffalo, elk, deer, and boar—so that they could ride to the hunt there.

Cliff-smasher lifted the Tatra Mountains from underground, and in them he carved valleys as courses for rivers and streams. He sharpened the peaks with his mountaineer's ax so that the clouds would snag and fly off in tatters instead of gathering over the earth and drenching it with torrential rains.

Such were the unheard-of wonders described by the old one as she read from the book.

The hut became crowded with people, barely leaving room to move. They listened to these tales. They listened, not knowing which was more amazing: Oak-uprooter, who could pull up huge, spreading trees from the ground as if they were mere carrots, or Cliff-smasher, who could change the features of the Tatra Mountains with his ax, or the old woman, who could look at those little black marks, small as buckwheat kernels, and read such incredible stories from them!

A deep dusk had fallen before the listeners remembered that they had work to do and began returning to their huts.

And the miller's wife, an intelligent woman, though lacking any book-learning, said to the old one, "Grandmother, why should you roam from village to village in this foul weather, through those puddles? Winter is coming. Snow, wind, and frost are coming. All the harsh weather hostile to man and beast is coming. Stay here at the mill for the winter. We'll give you a warm room, we'll give you food, and in return you'll teach my daughters to read from books."

And so, like this and like that, and this and that, they came to an agreement.

The old woman stayed.

In the first week the eldest daughter went for her lessons, but lessons weren't on her mind! She spun around in the old woman's room and said, "I'll be back, granny, in just a minute, as soon as I tend to the pig that got into some mischief!"

She ran out of the mill and didn't return until evening. She'd gone to a neighbor's to look at new clothes.

And the old woman dozed by the stove while the mother thought that her daughter was studying.

So it was each day with the eldest daughter, from Sunday to Sunday.

The second week came, and the middle daughter went for her lessons. She, too, spun around in the little room and called out, "I'll be back, granny, in just a minute, as soon as I hang the laundry to dry on the fence!"

She left and didn't return until evening, for she'd heard music at the neighbors' across the bridge.

And the old woman dozed by the stove while the mother thought that her daughter was studying.

So it was each day with the middle daughter, from Sunday to Sunday.

The third week came, and the youngest daughter went for her lessons.

And until dusk drove her from the book, she couldn't tear herself away. She was constantly asking about the letters.

"Tell me, granny, how is this little sign pronounced? And this one, like a circle? And this one, like a hook? And this one, twisted like a pig's tail?"

She brought a piece of smooth wax and wrote out the letters on the flat surface with a stick. When a week had gone by, she could read somewhat.

Time passed, and springtime came.

The older sisters hadn't learned anything from the old woman, but the youngest one could read like a wonder! From top to bottom, and from

bottom to top, whichever word she was shown, no matter how long, she could tell in a flash what it meant!

The word spread far and wide about the miller's daughters, about their beauty, their high spirits, and their learning.

The tidings reached an enchanter.

The enchanter thought to himself, *I must marry one of the miller's daughters. Each one of them is ravishing, and it will be a pleasure to gaze upon her beauty. Each one is merry, and it will be a delight to hear her laughter and her songs. Each one is learned and could well manage my household.*

And this enchanter was so ugly that he was a fright! He was tall and skinny as a beanpole, with a long scraggly beard, ears like a bat's, and a nose like a puffball.

The enchanter got dressed as a traveling peddler. He wore a short jacket in a foreign style, leather boots on his feet, and a box full of wares on his back.

He stood by the mill calling, "Ribbons for sale! Beads for sale! Perfumes for sale!"

The miller's eldest daughter ran out of the house. "Come here on the porch! Show me your wares, show me!"

The peddler went up. He took the box off his back and opened it. He brought out all sorts of trinkets, and he spread them out on the bench: handkerchiefs, bangles, ribbons, pins, buttons, beads, rings, fragrant soaps. They beamed bright as a rainbow and smelled sweet as a rose.

The miller's daughter's eyes shone. Her hands trembled at such beautiful things. She bought as many baubles as she could.

The peddler put the rest away. He closed the box and tied it to his back and said, "Kind maiden, walk me to the crossroads, for I don't know the shortest way."

The miller's daughter went with the peddler, and when they reached the crossroads, the enchanter reached into his pocket. He took out a golden apple, and he said, "Take this, dear girl, in return for your favor—a golden apple. But you must catch it yourself."

And he threw the apple down on the path.

The apple rolled away, and the miller's daughter ran after it.

Almost, almost . . . she was just about to grasp it, but the apple slipped

out of her hand and rolled further. It rolled by way of a road, a road, a field, a field, a wood, a wood . . . and it stopped at the edge of an abyss.

The miller's daughter leaned down and caught the apple, but she lost her balance and slid into the depths!

She fell and fell until she reached the bottom of the abyss. But she wasn't bruised at all.

She got up and looked around, and there stood a magnificent castle! It had marble walls, crystal windows, and a silver roof. And at her side stood the same peddler who had been at the mill.

"I am not a peddler, but an enchanter. This is my castle. I am the master here. You will stay here with me and you will manage my household. And if you are obedient, I will marry you. Come and see how splendidly you will live."

The enchanter led the miller's daughter through the chambers, where the furnishings were sumptuous, with each room more magnificent than the rest. The walls were painted, the floors were strewn with bearskins, carpets lay on the benches, silver vessels stood on the tables.

"You may go anywhere you like, look at yourself in all the mirrors, take clothes out of all the chests and dress up in them."

He took the miller's daughter to the dining room.

"Whatever you order to eat or drink will immediately appear on this table."

He walked her to the end of the hall. He stood before a closed door.

"Beyond this door is a room, a room that you may not enter. Remember this. If you disobey, you will be punished."

Then the enchanter disappeared, and the miller's daughter stayed alone in the beautiful castle.

The miller's eldest daughter had never liked working, so the life at the castle pleased her well.

She ran through the chambers. She changed her clothes constantly, always tying a new scarf on her head and standing in front of a mirror, enraptured by her own beauty. When she was hungry, she would go to the dining room, sit at the table, unfold her napkin, and make her wishes known. Whatever she ordered immediately appeared on the table before her.

After some time passed, the girl tired of doing nothing but dressing up. After all, who could see her in these fine clothes? No one, of course.

She stood in the hall before the closed door and thought to herself, *What could there possibly be in that room? Why did the enchanter forbid me to look? Eh, I'll look, just a quick peek!*

Here I should mention that the miller's daughter always carried the golden apple that the enchanter had given her.

She looked in.

She saw cage after cage, and in each one a bird. All the birds were sad, with hanging heads and drooping wings. In the center of the room stood a table. On the table lay a book sealed with seven seals.

"Eh, nothing interesting here! What do I care for birds? What do I care for books?"

So she left the room and closed the door behind her.

"He won't know that I was there."

A little time passed. Rumbling wheels approached the castle, a carriage drove up, and out of the carriage stepped the enchanter.

"Tell me, dear girl, what did you do here?"

"I amused myself by running through the chambers, singing songs, and stringing beads on a silken thread."

"Did you enter the forbidden room?"

"No . . . I didn't."

"Show me the apple!"

The miller's daughter took the golden apple out from her bosom, and it was covered with black spots. It was rotten and decayed.

"See what happened to the apple? You lied! The golden apple always shows me the truth. You did what I forbade—you looked into the room. You will be punished for it."

And he locked the girl in a shed.

Then he said to himself, "I must still decide what to turn her into, but first I'll ride off for the miller's second daughter, as soon as I change my clothes."

And the enchanter dressed as a rich nobleman. He shaved his beard and waxed his mustache. He put on a shirt fastened with buttons of gold, and over the shirt a silk jacket, blue in color. On his head he placed a pointed bearskin cap with an egret plume, and he pinned the plume to the cap with a diamond brooch. He girded himself with a heavy gold belt worked in four ornate designs, and he hung a scimitar from the belt. On his feet he wore shoes of red Moroccan leather, for, in the words of the song:

Water flows,
Cool breeze blows,
Black shoes for working,
Red shoes for dancing.

It's true indeed that he was ugly, and incredibly so! But it's also true that his costume was eye-catching.

The enchanter left his underground kingdom and rode for the mill.

And the miller's middle daughter happened to be standing by the pond. She was calling the ducklings to come out of the water, for she had brought them some food.

Her hair gleamed like copper in the setting sun. Her eyes were green and mysterious as the water splashing around her slender legs.

The enchanter was entranced by the girl. He tore the bearskin cap from his head, he bowed low to the ground before her, and he said, "Greetings, fair lady! I'm on my way to my brother's wedding, and a small accident has befallen me. The rim has come off a wheel of my carriage. I need a black-smith to help me. . . . Direct me to the forge, kind maiden."

"I'll take you there myself, noble sir."

The miller's daughter was thrilled at the thought of being seen in the village with such a well-dressed nobleman. She threw the bowl of food to the ground, took off her apron, and said, "Come follow me toward the milldam."

When they passed the dam, the enchanter said, "Don't trouble yourself anymore, gentle maiden, just point out with your hand which of the village houses is the blacksmith's."

And when the middle daughter showed him the house, he took the golden apple from his jacket pocket and he said, "Accept this apple, lovely maiden, as my thanks for your kindness. Oh . . . it fell from my hand! Oh . . . it's rolling downhill! Chase after it, dear girl, or it will fall into the water! Catch it for yourself, catch it!"

And the same thing happened as the last time.

The apple rolled away, and the miller's daughter ran after it.

Almost, almost . . . she was just about to grasp it, but the apple slipped out of her hand and rolled further. It rolled by way of a road, a road, a field, a field, a wood, a wood . . . and it stopped at the edge of an abyss.

The miller's daughter leaned down and caught the apple, but lost her balance and slid into the depths!

She saw before her a magnificent castle, and at her side stood the nobleman in the silk jacket, the same man she had led to the dam.

And the enchanter led this miller's daughter through the castle.

"You may go anywhere except into the room behind this door. Remember this."

Then he asked, "What do you like the most?"

"Most of all I like to dance."

"Well, then, take this magic box. When you turn the handle, the box will play and play, and you can dance."

Then the enchanter disappeared, and the miller's daughter was left alone in the huge castle.

The middle one had never liked work much, either, so she enjoyed life at the castle.

She ran through the chambers, she ate delicious meals, she dressed in beautiful clothes, and from time to time she wound up the box and danced and danced. . . .

But finally she grew tired of this, and she, too, looked into the forbidden room.

She saw the birds. She saw the book.

"Eh, what do I care about that?"

She left the room and closed the door behind her.

"He won't know that I was there."

A little time passed. The enchanter returned and he asked, "What did you do here, dear girl?"

"I ran through the chambers, I wound up the magic box, and I danced round and round."

"Did you look into the forbidden room?"

"No . . . I didn't."

"Show me the apple!"

The miller's daughter took the golden apple out from her bosom, and it was covered with black spots. It was decayed and rotten.

"You lied! See what happened to the apple? The golden apple always shows me the truth. You did what I forbade—you looked into the room. You will be punished for it."

And he locked the girl in a shed.

Then he said to himself, "I must still decide what to turn her into, but first I'll ride off for the miller's third daughter, as soon as I change my clothes."

The enchanter dressed as a beggar. On his feet he wore sandals fastened with bent twigs, on his back a muddy coat. He carried a sack of bread, and in one hand a stick wrapped with hedgehog skin to drive away unfriendly dogs.

And he went to the mill as an old beggar man.

The miller's youngest daughter brought him a piece of rye bread. The old man put the bread in his sack, he thanked the girl, and he said politely, "Kind maiden, walk me across the courtyard, for my eyesight is poor, and I'm afraid of falling in the well."

The youngest daughter didn't know how her sisters had disappeared. She didn't know that she was talking to an enchanter.

"I'll walk with you, grandfather."

And on the road just past the gate, the old man suddenly dropped the golden apple as if by accident, and he called out, "Ah, my little apple! It gave me such joy! It rolled into the grass! It'll get lost! I'll never find it!"

"Don't despair, grandfather! I'll fetch your apple!"

And the miller's daughter ran after the apple.

It rolled by way of a road, a road, a field, a field, a wood, a wood . . . and it stopped at the edge of an abyss.

The miller's daughter leaned down and caught the apple, but lost her balance and slid into the depths!

She wasn't bruised at all, and she got up right away. She saw a huge castle before her.

"What does this mean? Where am I?"

Then she heard laughter behind her. "Heh, heh, heh . . . you're surprised. . . ."

The girl looked around. She saw a tall man, skinny as a beanpole. His beard was long and scraggly, his ears like a bat's, his nose like a puffball— the very likeness of the old man to whom she had given a slice of bread, but differently dressed.

"I am not a beggar, but the lord of this castle. I will also tell you that I am an enchanter. You must stay here with me. You must live in this castle."

The miller's daughter was trembling with fear.

He must have captured my older sisters, she thought, *and now he's caught me, too. They never returned and I'll never return. . . . Oh, woe is me!*

She thought of her father and mother. Her parents stood before her eyes. They had cried after the older daughters and had wrung their hands. They had looked for them in neighboring villages, in forests and fields, and they hadn't found them anywhere.

Now they've lost me, too! she thought. *This will be the final blow. They'll never live through this. They won't survive!*

The enchanter led the miller's daughter through the castle. He showed her the splendid chambers, and he promised her a life of happiness.

But the miller's daughter didn't look at anything. Nothing interested her. Nothing cheered her up.

The enchanter didn't mention the forbidden room, for he thought to himself, *Even if she looks in that room, I'll keep her. I won't find a more beautiful bride in the whole wide world.*

The enchanter left his kingdom to perform wicked and villainous deeds, and the miller's youngest daughter stayed in the huge castle alone.

She didn't play or make merry like her older sisters. She didn't run through the chambers or gaze at herself in the mirrors or wind up the music box.

She wrung her fair hands and cried out her blue eyes thinking of her parents' misfortune, of the fate of her older sisters, and of her own fate as well.

Tired with sorrow and grief, she cried herself to sleep. And when she awoke, she thought, *Crying won't help a thing. I must look for a way to escape. I must flee from here.*

As she walked from chamber to chamber, she saw that all doors to the outside were locked, and all windows were bolted with iron bars.

Walking from place to place, she entered the forbidden room.

She saw the sad birds in their cages. Being kindhearted to all living things, she forgot her own sadness and took pity on the birds.

"Oh, you poor creatures! Shut in those cramped little cages, locked in those prisons of wire! You have neither food nor water!"

And then the birds awoke as if from a dream. They lifted their heads. They moved their wings.

"We heard the words of pity plain,
We want to live again! To live again!"

The miller's daughter was astounded. Wonder of wonders! Birds talking like people! So she called out, "What kind of magic birds are you that you speak in human tongues?"
And the birds said in unison:

"Though we have feathers, birds we're not,
But each a girl the old man caught.
Peasant daughters all are we,
Turned to birds, as you can see.

"Summers, winters come and go,
We sit locked up, full of woe.
Springtimes pass, autumns pass,
When will we be saved at last?"

And from the corner she heard familiar voices:

"Here we are, come and see,
Your own two sisters! Set us free!"

The miller's daughter ran to the corner, and there in a tiny cage two nightingales were fluttering and reaching out to her with their beaks. "Save us! Save us!"
The miller's daughter wrung her hands, and her eyes filled with tears.
"However can I save you? However can I break the spell? The cages have no doors, and all doors in the castle are locked. We'll never get out! We'll all perish here!"
And the birds answered in chorus:

"How to open the doors of our cages
Is explained in the magic book's pages.
If you can read the words in the book,
You'll learn how to free us, so hurry and look!"

The miller's daughter looked around. She saw a thick book, sealed with seven clasps, lying on a table.

The miller's daughter quickly unfastened the clasps and opened the book. She searched and searched, and then she found it! On the page with a picture of a lock it was written:

> If you wish to open a chest, cage, door, or whatever is locked, take the magic blade of grass, hold it against the closed object, and say these words:
>
> > "You are proud—humble yourself.
> > "You are closed—open yourself.
>
> > "So I command you for the first time, for the second time, and for the third time."

On the page lay a dried blade of grass.

Could this be the magic blade of grass?

The miller's daughter picked it up. She held the grass against the first cage, she spoke the magic words, and the cage opened up!

What luck! What joy!

Quickly, quickly . . . she held the grass against the second cage, against the third. . . . She opened them all! The happy birds flew out of the cages and sat in a row on the window ledge. They turned their heads, and they flapped their wings.

"Look further! Read further!"

The miller's daughter searched and searched in the book. Ah, here was a page with a picture of a nightingale. And on this page was written:

> If you wish to turn a person into a bird, stand facing the east, turn on your heel three times from left to right, and say these words:
>
> > "Edzhubedzhu chamuray!
> > Words which cast a spell say I.
> > Your appearance has changed.
> > Tlan-ran-zird,
> > You are now a bird!"
>
> If you wish to reverse the spell and turn the bird back into a person, do and say all of this backwards.

One-two-three the miller's daughter stood facing the west, she turned three times on her toes from right to left, and she said:

"Bird a now are you,
Zird-ran-tlan,
Changed has appearance your,
I say spell a cast which words,
Chamuray edzhubedzhu!

And still another wonder took place! The twenty birds had disappeared. Twenty maidens were standing around the miller's daughter in a circle! Twenty maidens clapped their hands, smiling, rejoicing!

And the miller's daughter urged them on. "Let us flee! Let us flee before the enchanter returns!"

She seized the huge book, she took the magic blade of grass, and she ran out of the room, with the maidens after her, after her!

The miller's daughter touched one door after another with the blade of grass, and she spoke the magic words. Locks crumbled, latches fell, doors swung open.

In such a way nine doors opened, nine window grates crumbled, nine gates stood wide. And beyond the ninth gate were the forests of the real world, familiar fields, and the villages of home.

At once the maidens dispersed in all four directions to their huts.

And the miller's three daughters ran home to the mill.

Hurrying, hurrying, they passed the crossroads, they passed the milldam, they walked through the gate.

Suddenly they heard a clamor behind!

The enchanter was after them!

The miller's youngest daughter set the book on a bench as fast as possible and opened it. She chanced on the page with a picture of a mouse. Quickly she scanned it with her eyes. She picked three leaves, and then she read the magic words:

"'Hocus-pocus shoomie-bine,
Listen to these words of mine.
Three leaves in a cross, I face my house,
May the enchanter turn into a mouse!'"

The enchanter was already in the courtyard!

But once the spell was cast, the tall man began to shrink and shrink . . . and shrink . . . until he turned into a little gray mouse.

Then the miller's cat, who had been sunning himself on the porch, pounced, caught the mouse, strangled it, and ate it!

And so the evil enchanter met his end.

His castle collapsed at once and sank seventy miles into the center of the earth, leaving no trace behind.

The miller's daughter sent the enchanted book, by way of raftsmen sailing down the Vistula to Gdansk, to the king in the Wawel Castle.

To this day the book is kept in the castle of the printed word, fastened by a chain to its table.

But it has lost its magical powers.

The enchanted blade of grass crumbled to dust seven centuries ago, and the wind scattered the dust all over the world.